The Goat-skin Lad

and Other Tales

Retold by
Martin Waddell

Illustrated by Steve Cox

Contents

The Goat-skin Lad

There was once a small skinny scrap of a lad called Tomas Maguire. He was famous around Ennis because he went about dressed in a goat-skin.

Why did he go round dressed like a goat?

His mother was poor. She had no clothes to put him in, until her old black and white goat died. Then she took the goat-skin and made Tomas a kind of a goat-dress.

'I look like a goat!' Tomas complained.

'It's better than no clothes at all,' the widow replied.

He finished up the stew she had made from the rest of the goat and then he went out ... in the goat-skin.

The neighbours knew that the widow's old goat had died and they laughed when they saw Tomas in the goat-skin.

'Maguire's old goat is back from the dead on two legs!' they told each other. There was nothing the lad in the goat-skin could do but grin back and join in the goat jokes.

One day Tomas was out in the wood getting sticks for the fire. Then … CLUMP! CLUMP! CLUMP! Along came a Giant, with a big club.

The Giant saw what looked like a skinny black and white goat at his feet.

'Here's lunch!' thought the Giant.

He took a swing at the goat with his club.

Tomas didn't just look like a goat, he was nimble as a goat as well (maybe because of all the goat stew he'd been eating).

When he heard the swish of the club coming down, he jumped to one side.

WALLOP! went the club on the ground.

The club bounced back and tapped the Giant lightly on the forehead. The Giant went down like a log and was knocked out cold.

Tomas couldn't understand how the tiny tap had knocked the Giant out, but he didn't stop to think about it. He tied the Giant up with the rope that he used for dragging sticks.

When the Giant came round, Tomas was standing over him holding the club. It was such a big club that he could only just lift it.

'Don't hit me!' screamed the Giant. 'That club was made by the fairies. It is magic. One hard blow with that will kill anyone.'

'Is that so?' said Tomas, as though he was thinking of killing the giant.

'Spare me and … and … I'll let you keep the club!' roared the Giant. 'Giant's Honour I will!'

'It's a deal,' Tomas said, and he untied the Giant.

The Giant ran off into the wood.

Now the Giant was big, but his two brothers were bigger. One had two heads, the other had three.

The Giant had given his word of honour to let Tomas have the club, but that didn't stop his brothers trying to get it back for him. No Giant likes losing a one-hard-blow-and-you're-dead magic club.

When Tomas went out to get firewood again, the two-headed Giant was waiting for him. He had two beards that grew down to his feet, like ivy, and legs like oak trees.

Tomas saw the legs but he thought they were trees. He was standing between the two trees, when one of the branches suddenly dipped.

The Giant reached down to grab him, but Tomas was quick as a goat. He skipped out of the way of the Giant's big hand.

The Giant spun round to catch him ... and tripped.

Tomas tapped him with the club. The Giant was knocked out cold. A *tap* was all it was, not a *wallop*, for Tomas hadn't the heart of a killer in him.

'Spare me!' wailed the Giant when he came round.

'Well, I might, if you make it worth my while,' said Tomas.

'I'll give you my flute,' bargained the Giant. 'How would that be?'

'A flute isn't much,' Tomas answered.

'It's a magic flute,' said the Giant. 'Tootle a note on that and everyone will dance, whether they want to or not!'

So Tomas went off with the flute.

The Giant ran away to fetch the third brother, the three-headed one.

CLUMP! CLUMP! CLUMP! The three-headed Giant came into the wood. He was bigger than both of his brothers, and nastier.

This time, Tomas was ready.

The Giant was looking North, South and West with his heads as he came through the wood.

Tomas hid up a tree to the East.
And

tap!

tap!

tap!

Tomas tapped all three heads
one by one as they passed. The
Giant was knocked out cold like his
brothers.

'I've my club from your one-
headed brother, and my flute from the
brother with two heads. What will you
give me to spare you?' Tomas asked
when the Giant came round.

'I'll give you my jar of green
ointment!' the three-headed Giant
replied.

'An old jar of ointment?' said
Tomas. 'What good is that?' He raised
the club high over his head, as though
he was about to strike.

'Wait!' screamed all three heads in a chorus. 'Put this ointment on and you'll never be scalded or burned, whatever else happens.'

'That sounds good to me,' Tomas said. 'But there's to be no more killing round here, or anywhere else. That goes for you and your two brothers.'

'But killing is what Giants do!' wailed the three heads.

'In that case, you'll be a dead Giant,' said Tomas. 'Now which of your heads will I bang first with my club?'

'STOP!' wailed the heads. 'It's a deal!'

That left Tomas with a club that could win any fight, a flute that could make the world dance, and an ointment that spared him from scalds and burns.

'I suppose they'll be useful,' thought Tomas. But he didn't know just how useful they'd turn out to be.

One day news came from Dublin.

The King wanted his daughter to marry a prince. Lots of them came to his court. They wanted to marry the Princess and share her fortune. But she didn't like any of them.

'I'll put on a grim face, and that will put them all off,' she told herself. And for seven long years she sat there without smiling or laughing or even a grin.

'Here's what I'll do,' thought the King. And he made it known that he'd let the girl marry the first man who could make her laugh three times. He made it three times, because he didn't want her to marry some horrible prince who made her laugh by mistake.

Tomas set off to win the Princess. He turned up at the gates of the Palace, in his goat-skin, and stated his business.

'Who do you think you are?' laughed the guards at the gate. 'A lad in a smelly old goat-skin, turning up here to wed the King's daughter. Get out of here! You must be mad.'

Tap-tap-tap, Tomas went with his club, and the guards ended up in the moat.

Tomas went into the King's Court.

'I've come here to wed the Princess!' Tomas told the King. Everyone thought he was joking.

The Princes were dressed in fine clothes to impress the Princess. When they saw Tomas they laughed because Tomas looked such a mess in his goat-skin.

'Get out!' they said.

'Not till I've had my chance with the Princess!' Tomas replied.

The Princess smiled … but she stopped herself laughing just in time.

No one noticed the smile except for one man, Prince Ruari-the-Red. Ruari wanted to marry the Princess himself.

'This lad has only come here to make you look foolish!' he told the King. 'You'd not have your daughter wed to a goat!'

Everyone laughed, except the Princess … and Tomas.

'Let him prove himself and take some of us on!' Ruari said. 'We'll make minced meat of the goat!'

Ruari didn't tackle Tomas himself, just in case. He let another man have a go first. This man was a fierce looking prince, all dressed in gold, with a sword that was sharp as a needle.

Tap, went Tomas with his club, gently enough.

The Prince fell on the floor with his head ringing.

More princes tried, one after the other, but Tomas knocked them over, just like that.

Then seven of them tackled Tomas, all at the same time. Seven at once made no difference to Tomas. He knocked them all down, one by one.

They lay on the floor, moaning and groaning.

'Any more for the goat?' Tomas asked with a grin. And that's when the Princess *laughed* at the sight of all the brave Princes laid out on the floor around small skinny Tomas.

'That's the first laugh!' Tomas told the King. 'Two laughs to go.' That didn't please Ruari.

'If the goat is so brave,' he said, 'let's see how he copes with the huge wolf who's been eating our cattle!'

The King thought Ruari's idea was good. He wanted to be rid of the huge wolf.

'But … but the poor lad will be killed by the wolf!' cried the Princess, going pale.

'Don't worry, Princess!' Tomas said. 'Just show me the huge wolf, and I'll settle the matter … but take care to cover your ears when he comes.'

'What for?' asked the Princess.

'Just take my tip, do it,' said Tomas.

The next day, the huge wolf appeared.

'I'll bite off your head!' the wolf growled, showing a mouthful of enormous teeth.

'Toot-toot!' went small skinny Tomas on his flute.

The wolf started dancing, and he couldn't stop. All the others around were set dancing too, including Ruari-the-Red. They danced so fast that their legs hurt.

All except the Princess. She kept her hands over her ears, and so she didn't dance … though her feet tapped a bit.

The Princes danced and pranced, yelling at Tomas to stop playing. They looked so funny that the Princess laughed.

Tomas didn't stop playing until the huge wolf danced away over the mountains.

'That's two laughs!' Tomas told the King.

'Hold on!' Ruari said. 'It takes *three* laughs to win the Princess!'

'I'm working on that!' said small skinny Tomas.

'Well, here's *my* plan!' said Ruari. 'The Man Down Below has a whip that would help us to defeat the Vikings when they come raiding. Let Tomas prove himself by bringing it here to the King.'

'Great idea!' the King told Tomas.

The Princess didn't laugh this time. She thought Tomas would be killed by the Man Down Below.

'I'll marry you anyway,' she said to Tomas. 'I don't want you to risk your life for me.'

'Three laughs it was!' Ruari said quickly.

'This is no laughing matter!' the Princess wept.

'Never mind, Princess dear,' said Tomas. 'I've a trick or two that will soon put the Man Down Below in his place.'

I don't know just where Down Below was, or how the small skinny lad in the goat-skin got there, but somehow he found it. There was the Man Down Below and the whip.

'I've come to borrow your whip,' Tomas said. 'The King of Dublin sent me for it, so he could beat off the Vikings.'

'Is that so?' said the Man Down Below. He laid it down on the ground before Tomas.

'Pick it up, Tomas!' he said, with a grin.

The whip was red-hot to the touch and Tomas knew it. That's where the green ointment came in. Tomas had covered himself with the stuff.

Tomas picked up the whip, and the Man Down Below quickly stopped laughing. He started cursing instead.

'Thank you kindly, good sir!' Tomas said, and off he went with the whip.

'The whip, sire!' Tomas said to the King of Dublin. He laid the whip on the floor by the feet of the King.

That was too much for Ruari-the-Red. He grabbed the whip to beat Tomas with it …

The red hot whip burned his hand. He howled, but Tomas was quick with the ointment. He didn't want to see anyone hurt, so he took away all of the pain.

Ruari made a terrible fuss, and cried like a baby who wanted his mother. He stamped his feet and pulled silly faces.

The King started laughing. So did everyone else ... including the Princess!

'That's three laughs. I claim the Princess!' Tomas told the King. Before the King could answer, the Princess nipped off her throne and she kissed the goat-lad.

That's how Tomas Maguire won his Princess.

When the Princess married Tomas, she wore a goat-skin as white as the snow on the mountains. She looked lovely.

Tomas still looked (just a bit) like a goat!

Dan and the Leprechaun's Gold

There once was a shifty-eyed rogue of a thief named Dan Smart, who lived in the townland of Pogue. He told people that he fixed pots and pans, pretending that he was a good honest tinker.

'I *tink* this and *tink* that,' he'd say with a sly grin, but wherever he went he took this and took that, for stealing was his way of making a living.

One day, Dan stole a pig from Crusty Malone's farm. Dan ran off down the lane with Crusty behind him, waving a stick.

Crusty was much faster than Dan. Crusty soon got back his pig … but he wasn't finished with Dan.

He took a saucepan from the pack on Dan's back and stuck it over Dan's head.

'Tink your way out of that, Dan!' Crusty said.

Dan blundered about in the lane. He wound up in a ditch full of mud.

'Help me someone!' cried Dan. Then he heard the sound of a tinker's hammer.

Tink tink tink tink.

'Is that a tinker?' Dan shouted.

'Well … a kind of a tinker,' said someone.

'*Tink* this saucepan off my head with your hammer, please!' Dan wailed from the ditch.

'No sooner asked than it's done,' said the voice.

Tink tink tink tink … off came the saucepan.

'I'm greatly obliged,' Dan said, rubbing his ears.

The little gentleman was as small as the saucepan. He had brown eyes like nutmegs, an apron of leather, and a curly hat with a red ribbon wound round the brim.

'You're a leprechaun!' Dan gasped.

He fixed his eyes on the little gentleman, for he knew that if you take your eyes off a leprechaun, he can disappear in a flash.

'Well, what if I am?' said the little gentleman.

Dan was covered in mud, and he hadn't a penny … but here was his chance to get money. All leprechauns have a pot of gold. If he could lay his hands on the Leprechaun's gold, he would be a rich man, forever.

He grabbed the Leprechaun round the throat.

'Let me go!' said the little gentleman. 'This is small thanks for my work!' He struggled so much that his hat fell off him, but he couldn't escape from Dan's grip.

'I've my eyes fixed on you!' Dan warned him. 'Promise to show me the way to your pot of gold, and I'll let go of your throat.'

'If I must, I must,' the little

gentleman sighed. 'I promise to show you the way to my gold, and I always do what I promise.'

'Well show me!' said Dan, letting go of the little gentleman's throat.

'That's the road we must take,' the little gentleman said, and he pointed. Dan turned to look where he'd pointed.

'I've fooled you, Dan,' laughed the little gentleman. 'I'm not letting you tink my gold!'

Then he vanished, like *that*, in a flash, as all leprechauns can when they have to. Dan was left holding the Leprechaun's hat with the red ribbon wound round the brim. And the saucepan was back on Dan's head!

He followed the hedge all the way home, stumbling and blundering along. He found some soap and he soaped himself well.

Next, Dan stood on his head till the soap flowed down into the saucepan. Then he stood up and he pulled with both hands … and the saucepan slipped over his ears.

Dan got his head out of the saucepan … though it left him with cauliflower ears.

He looked at the hat with the red ribbon wound round the brim. 'I'm not beat yet!' Dan decided. 'That little gentleman will come back for his hat tomorrow night … and that's when I'll nab him.'

The next night he went back to the road where he'd first heard the *tinking*. He laid the hat with the red ribbon on it down by the hedge. Then he hid behind the hedge with the saucepan held ready.

'I know he's just saucepan size. When he reaches out for the hat, I'll slam down the saucepan and trap him!' thought Dan.

The moon rose … and Dan was still hiding there with the saucepan, watching the hat. Then he heard someone coming along.

'Where's my hat? Where's my hat?' the someone muttered.

Dan raised the saucepan.

'There's my hat!' the little gentleman said, reaching out for the hat with the red ribbon round it.

WHAM! Down came the saucepan. It covered the little gentleman from his head to his knees.

'Get out of that!' Dan told the little gentleman.

The dancing saucepan with the little gentleman in it skipped and bounced, twisting this way and that. All Dan could see were the little gentleman's legs sticking out at the bottom.

'I've outsmarted you this time!' Dan boasted.

'You're too smart for me, Dan!' the little gentleman grunted.

'Who's the fool now?' gloated Dan. 'Which way do we go to get hold of your gold?'

'The way that I showed you before,' the little gentleman said slyly. 'Just look over there and you'll see the way you should go.'

'Nice one!' said Dan. 'You did that
before. I looked away and you
vanished. I'm not falling for that one
again.'

'There speaks a smart man,'
groaned the little gentleman.

'Lead me to your pot of gold!' Dan
said.

'With this saucepan on my head, I
can't see,' said the little gentleman.
'How can I show you the way?'

'I'm not falling for that,' said Dan.
'I have you safe in the saucepan. And
you're magic. Your feet know the way!'

'Well, I suppose I must,' said the little gentleman. 'But remember, once you lose sight of me for a moment … I'm gone. It's the way that I am. I can vanish as quick as a candle blows out.'

Dan and the saucepan went up the lane with the little gentleman's legs working hard, as they stuck out beneath the saucepan.

'Look over there, Dan,' said the little gentleman.

But Dan wouldn't look.

'There's a five pound note on the ground!' suggested the little gentleman, but Dan wouldn't take his eyes off him to look.

'Who's that beautiful girl over there?' asked the little gentleman.

Dan kept his eyes fixed on the little saucepan with legs.

'You're too smart for me, Dan,' the little gentleman said again.

Then he started to puff.

'What's wrong with you?' asked Dan.

'This saucepan is terribly heavy!'

the little gentleman sighed.

'Then sit for a minute,' said Dan.
'Take a rest and we'll go on as before.'

The little gentleman folded his
legs and sat down inside the saucepan.
Dan sat beside him, still looking at the
saucepan.

'Can you see my legs, Dan, now
I'm sitting down inside this saucepan?'
the little gentleman asked very
politely.

'Well … no,' said Dan.

'Now I've fooled you twice, Dan!'
the little gentleman laughed. 'I'm not
having you tink my gold.' And he
vanished again.

Somehow the saucepan was back on Dan's head, stuck quite as fast as before.

Dan blundered home again.

By the time it was off, he was covered in soap and hot water, and gurgling with anger as though he would burst.

'I'll have him yet!' he swore angrily, for he had his heart set on getting the Leprechaun's gold.

The next day Dan stole a fisherman's net. 'The net's full of holes and I can see him inside it, not like the saucepan,' he thought.

He laid the hat on the road as before, but this time Dan hid up a tree.

The little gentleman came down the road just after dusk. He looked at the hat.

'Are you there, Dan?' he said to the hedge, where Dan had hidden before.

Of course Dan said nothing.

'Here I am. There's my hat and no Dan,' said the little gentleman. And he reached out for the hat with the red ribbon on it.

WOOOOOOOOOOOOOOOOOSH! Down came the net on the little gentleman.

'This time I've got you!' Dan crowed.

'You're too smart for me, Dan!' the little gentleman said.

'Take me to the spot where the gold's buried. That spot and no other!' said Dan.

Dan picked up the net with the little gentleman inside. He stuck the hat with the red ribbon back on the little gentleman's head.

'Would you settle for half?' sighed the little gentleman, as they set off.

'No way!' said Dan.

He walked and he walked and he walked.

'Are you trying to walk my legs off?' muttered Dan, as they trudged through a field of ripe corn that shone yellow and bright by the light of the moon.

'I told you it was a long way,' said the little gentleman.

'You and your tricks!' muttered Dan. 'You're getting me lost, and you know it.'

'I'm leading you straight to the pot,' the little gentleman said.

He touched the top of a cornstalk.

'My pot of gold is buried here, right under this yellow cornstalk!' said the little gentleman.

'There's a trick in this somewhere,' thought Dan, but he couldn't think what the trick was.

'How deep is it buried?' asked Dan.

'It's ten metres or more underground,' said the little gentleman. 'Perhaps I could help you … but I've only my small hands to dig with.'

'I'm not falling for that. You're not digging!' said Dan.

'You're too smart for me, Dan,' said the little gentleman, looking sadder than sad, although there was a gleam in his eye. 'It's a pity you weren't smart enough to bring a spade with you.'

'Well, I didn't!' sneered Dan.

'Then do what you usually do,' suggested the little gentleman. 'Find the next farmer's place and sneak in and steal his best spade.'

'I'm not falling for that!' Dan said. 'By the time I get back … there'll be no pot of gold in this field!'

'I'll make you another promise,'
the little gentleman sighed. 'You know
I always do what I promise. I promise
I won't move the pot of gold. It will be
where it is now when you come back
in the morning, still buried beneath
this cornstalk.'

Dan looked at the cornfield in the
moonlight.

'I'm not falling for that!' Dan told the little gentleman. 'It is only one cornstalk in a field of ten thousand cornstalks … I'd never find it again.'

'You're too smart for me, Dan!' said the little gentleman. 'I thought I'd got you that time!'

'You bet I am smart!' said Dan, and he grabbed the little gentleman's hat off his head. He undid the red ribbon that wound round the brim, and stuffed the Leprechaun's hat in his pocket.

He tied the red ribbon to the cornstalk. 'Promise me you won't move that red ribbon before I come back!' he told the little gentleman, and the little gentleman promised.

Dan went off to steal someone's spade, leaving the little gentleman by the field. What Dan didn't see was the grin on the little gentleman's face.

Dan came back to the field the next morning. The sun shone on the field full of corn.

Ten thousand yellow cornstalks were there … and every one had a bright red ribbon tied to its head. The field that should have been gold was glowing bright red.

'The Leprechaun fooled me!' cried Dan. He danced and he screamed and he shouted with rage. 'A curse on that little gentleman.'

But the little gentleman had kept his promise, and his pot of gold.

All Dan had for his trouble were two cauliflower ears, a battered saucepan, and a leprechaun's hat in his pocket.

Which … just about … served him right!

Little Cornstalk

There was once a widow who had three sons. The two older ones were called Christy and Liam. The third one she called Little Cornstalk because he was small and had yellow hair.

Christy and Liam made their small brother do all the work, while they snoozed.

'Fetch the cows, Little Cornstalk!' Christy ordered.

'Plough the field, Little Cornstalk!' Liam told him.

'Feed the hens, Little Cornstalk!' said both the brothers.

It was work-all-the-day-for-nothing for Little Cornstalk, and he was fed up.

'I'll find someone who'll pay me to work,' he told his brothers.

Little Cornstalk went to the fair and met Skinflint McGraw, who was the meanest farmer in Ireland … but Little Cornstalk didn't know that.

'I'll pay you six pennies a day for three whole days. But if I have to sack you before the three days are up, you get nothing!'

Little Cornstalk thought for a moment.

'You can't sack me for doing what you tell me to do,' Little Cornstalk said very carefully. 'So long as I do it.'

'Of course not,' agreed Skinflint, with a sly grin.

'Then it's a deal!' said Little Cornstalk.

When Little Cornstalk told his brothers about working for Skinflint McGraw, they roared with laughter.

'Skinflint will work you till you burst, baby brother. You won't last one day, let alone three!' Christy crowed.

'He'll sack you without any pay!' chuckled Liam.

'Care to bet?' Little Cornstalk challenged them.

'Bet taken … if Skinflint pays you for three days, we'll do the work that you usually do for a year!' the two brothers chuckled. 'You'll need a rest when he's finished with you!'

On Little Cornstalk's first day at work, Skinflint said to him, 'I want you to dig all the cow muck out of the barn.'

'I'll do what you tell me to do,' said Little Cornstalk.

'He won't manage it!' Skinflint thought, with a grin. 'When he's done all he can do, I'll be able to sack him. His work won't have cost me a penny.'

Little Cornstalk dug the muck out of the barn. It was stinky and dirty and he had to work hard.

Soon the barn was as clean as it could be, and a big pile of muck lay steaming outside in the yard.

'*Job done!*' Little Cornstalk panted, wiping his brow. 'I've done a hard day's work for my pay!'

'That's only *half* your day's work,' Skinflint said quickly. 'Clear all that muck out of my yard. If you don't want to do it … then go. But of course you won't get any pay if you do.'

Little Cornstalk knew he'd been cheated … but two could play at that game.

'I'll do what you tell me to do,' he told Skinflint carefully. He set to work.

When Skinflint came out to inspect it, the dirty old farmyard was clean as a new pin.

'*Job done!*' said Little Cornstalk.

But when Skinflint opened the door of the barn …

... WOOOSH! He was covered in cow muck!

'You've piled all the cow muck back in the barn,' roared Skinflint. 'Get out! Go home! You're sacked!'

'I did exactly what you told me to,' Little Cornstalk replied. 'I cleared the muck out of the yard. If you sack me you have to pay me three days' wages!'

Skinflint saw that he had been tricked. He stormed off. 'I'll get my own back!' he told himself. 'Tomorrow I'll work Little Cornstalk so hard that he'll have to quit!'

The next morning he said to his wife, 'I'll set Little Cornstalk to thatch the whole roof. It'll take him all day to get the long grass cut from the bank of the stream. It'll take him all night to put it on the roof. Then I'll find some small fault in it, so that I can sack him. I'll have my new roof and it won't have cost me a penny.'

'It's a very big roof. I'll have to work hard all day to do that,' Little Cornstalk said, when Skinflint gave him his orders.

'Hard work is what I pay you for,' Skinflint said. Then he added cunningly, 'Do it so it would please your own mother!'

'I've trapped Little Cornstalk this time!' thought Skinflint.

But Little Cornstalk saw right through the trap. He knew what to do and he did it.

Skinflint and his wife went off to the market. When they came back, a brand new thatch gleamed on the

roof. It was made with good golden straw, not greeny-grey like the long grass from the bank of the stream.

'*Job done!*' said Little Cornstalk.

Then he showed Skinflint the bill for the straw.

'I can't afford thatch like that!' Skinflint gasped. 'Four loads of good straw, and the hire of four carts and four men to carry it here to my farm! I'll sack you for wasting my money!'

'You told me to do what would please my own mother … so I put on the best thatch that I could! My mother would love a straw thatch like that, though we could never afford it. We have to use the greeny-grey long grass from beside the stream,' Cornstalk replied. 'I did *exactly* what you told me to, and you can't sack me for that.'

Skinflint had been outwitted again, but he was determined not to be beaten.

He came up with a plan to settle Little Cornstalk for good. It was ruthless and cruel, but Skinflint didn't mind that … so long as it cost him no money.

'Go to the turf bog and cut turf tonight! You can work by the light of the moon. Don't come back to the farm till you've cut me six drills of fresh turf,' he ordered Little Cornstalk.

'I've worked hard all day,' Little Cornstalk said, yawning. 'I need my sleep and my supper. No one stays out on the turf bog after dark.'

'Day or night makes no difference when you're working for me!' Skinflint smirked. 'Take your supper with you!'

'He'll drown in one of the deep pools when he's walking back in the dark!' Skinflint thought to himself. 'I'll have all the turf we need cut for the winter. When the boy is found dead, it won't cost me a penny in wages!'

Little Cornstalk knew he could drown coming back over the turf bog after dark. He thought for a bit, then …

… he knew what to do, and he did it!

'Master says I'm to have my supper with me when I go to cut the turf,' he told Skinflint's wife.

She gave Little Cornstalk his supper in a paper bag. It wasn't good food, just stale bread and bad butter. Little Cornstalk opened the bag and ate the supper right there and then.

'I'm off to the turf bog and my supper's with me!' he told Skinflint's wife cheerfully, when he had finished his supper.

Then he picked up his turf cutter and went out to the turnip field where Skinflint was weeding the turnips.

'What are you doing here? Why aren't you at the turf bog where you're supposed to be?' Skinflint asked, thinking he'd found a reason to sack Little Cornstalk.

'I'm on my way now,' said Little Cornstalk, 'but tell me ... what am I to do after I've had my supper?'

'You go straight to bed after your supper!' Skinflint said angrily. 'What else would you do?'

'Well ... I suppose if that's what you want me to do, I must do it,' the boy said, looking doubtful.

'No ifs and buts ... do what I've just told you to do!' Skinflint barked.

Five hours went by and the cold moonlight shone over the farm. Little Cornstalk still hadn't come back.

'Just think of Little Cornstalk out on the turf bog,' chortled Skinflint, in the kitchen.

'But he can't be!' said Skinflint's wife, sounding puzzled. 'I heard him snoring just now in the stable!'

'Got Little Cornstalk this time!' crowed Skinflint. 'He *couldn't* go and cut turf and be back and tucked up in the stable already. He didn't go there at all! That means I can sack him!'

Skinflint went out to the stable, chuckling with delight. He brought a big stick with him to beat Little Cornstalk for all the trouble he'd caused.

'Get up, you rogue!' Skinflint roared, waving his stick over his head. 'You've broken our deal, and you're sacked!'

'You told me to go straight to bed after my supper,' Little Cornstalk said coolly. 'I'd *had* my supper … so I went to bed. *Job done*! I did *exactly* what you told me to. If you sack me for that you must pay me my three days' wages!'

Skinflint went red in the face. 'I'm not sacking you!' he yelled, and he went back to the house.

'I'm not beaten yet!' Skinflint growled to his wife. 'I'll find a way to cheat Little Cornstalk out of his three days' pay. Tomorrow is his third day and I'm not going to pay him anything!'

The next day Skinflint said to Little Cornstalk, 'The big black cow is missing. I want you to find her.'

'Where will I look for her, Master?' Little Cornstalk asked.

'Look *everywhere* till you find my black cow!' Skinflint said, rubbing his hands in delight. 'Don't argue with me, or I'll sack you.'

'I've told Little Cornstalk to find our black cow that is lost,' Skinflint told his wife.

'Black cow?' asked his wife. 'We haven't got a black cow.'

'And that's why he won't be able to find her,' laughed Skinflint with delight. 'I'll be able to sack him. That means I won't have to pay him a penny.'

Then it started to rain. The rain poured through the brand new thatch. It ran in streams down the walls and made puddles on the floor.

'What's going on here?' roared Skinflint, running out into the yard.

There was Little Cornstalk tearing
the expensive thatch off Skinflint's
new roof. The roof was half gone, and
the new straw lay scattered in the yard.

'Stop that!' Skinflint roared. 'You've
wrecked my new roof. What do you
think you are doing?'

'I'm looking for your black cow,' Little Cornstalk said, looking down. 'That's what you told me to do.'

'You won't find a cow in my thatch!' howled Skinflint. 'You're sacked!'

'You told me to look *everywhere*,' Little Cornstalk replied. 'And I'm doing exactly what you told me to do. *Job done*! You know you can't sack me for that without breaking our deal.'

'I … I … I …' Skinflint stuttered as he looked at his ruined thatch, his barn full of cow muck and his empty turf store.

'What would you like me to do next?' grinned Little Cornstalk.

'CLEAR OFF AND NEVER COME BACK!' roared the farmer.

'My money first!' said Little Cornstalk. 'I'm not going without my wages.'

'Getting rid of you is cheap at the price!' moaned old Skinflint. And he paid Little Cornstalk his wages.

Little Cornstalk ran home with a grin on his face.

'Here comes the worker!' joked Christy and Liam, when they saw him come running up the lane.

'I worked for three days!' said Little Cornstalk.

'We *knew* you'd say that!' laughed his brothers. 'You may think you are smart, but you're not smart enough to fool us. You quit on day one. You've been hiding somewhere ever since, afraid to come home and admit it.'

'I worked for three days!' Little Cornstalk insisted.

'All right! If you worked for three days, where's the three days' wages you earned from Skinflint?' asked his brothers. 'Remember our bet? If you were paid, we had to do all the work that you usually do for a year! But we know you lost! No one ever got money out of Skinflint!'

Then Little Cornstalk pulled his wages out of his pocket and put them on the table.

'*Job done!*' grinned Little Cornstalk.

Benny Green's
Cricket Archive